Olivia's
Doctor Adventures

by Dr. Ashley Denmark

Illustrations by Mike Motz

Thank you to my mom and dad for giving me wings to take flight in life.
I wouldn't be Dr. Denmark without you.

To my husband, Anthony. Thank you for being the perfect
puzzle piece to my life. Your love is everything.

To my beautiful children, Olivia, Ethan, and Vivian. You are my
light and bring me so much joy. Never forget the power inside
of you to achieve the impossible. Mommy loves you always.

To the children in my hometown, Jennings, Missouri. You are smart,
you are talented, and you are capable of conquering the world.
Never let anyone tell you different.

Olivia's
Doctor Adventures

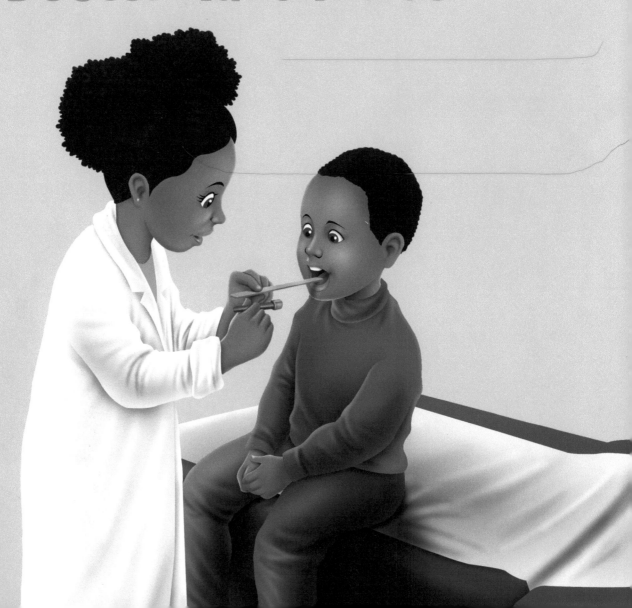

"Mommy's home!" shouts Olivia with glee.

"Hello, everyone. I missed you guys all day!"
says Mother.

"Mommy, how was your day at work? How many patients did you see in clinic?" Olivia eagerly asks.

"I was busy all day, but it was great. I love seeing my patients and helping them feel better!" Mother responds.

"What do doctors do, Mommy?" Olivia asks.

"Doctors help take care of people when they are sick and try to make sure people stay as healthy as possible," Mother replies.

"When I grow up, can I become a doctor like you?" Olivia asks her mom.

"Yes! If you work hard, you can become anything you want, including a doctor," says Mother happily.

"What kind of doctor can I be, Mommy?"
Olivia asks.

You can be a cardiologist. Cardiologists take care of your heart. If someone has a heart that skips a beat or makes a strange noise called a murmur, they can fix it.

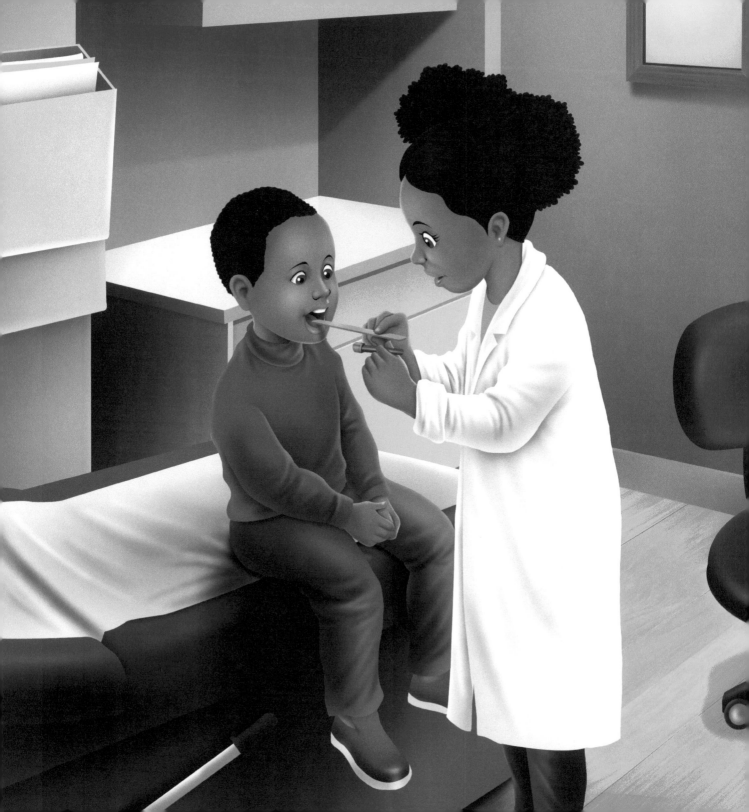

Or you can be a pediatrician. They take care of babies, kids, and teenagers. They will help you when you are sick, and they will also help you stay healthy so you can run and play.

Family medicine doctors take care of everyone in your family including your sisters, brothers, mom, dad, and even your grandparents. These doctors can do many things including wellness exams, fixing cuts, sports exams, and delivering babies.

———————⋅◦⟨⟨⟨⟩⟩⟩◦⋅———————

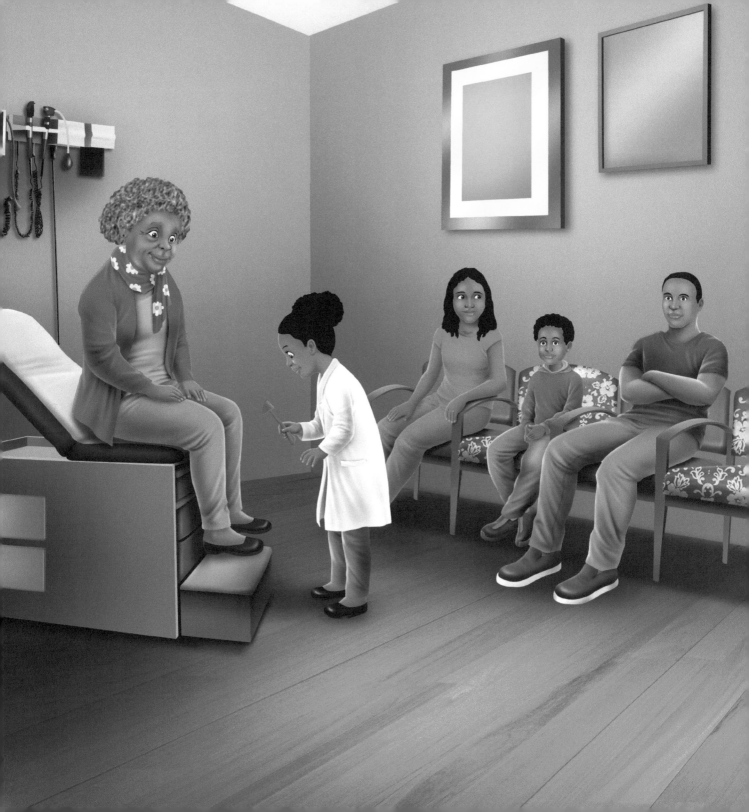

You can be an orthopedic surgeon. They are often called the bone doctors. They take care of your bones, joints, and muscles. If someone breaks a bone, they can fix it.

You can also be a psychiatrist. They help people deal with feelings including sadness, anger, shyness, or worrying. They find ways to make people happy.

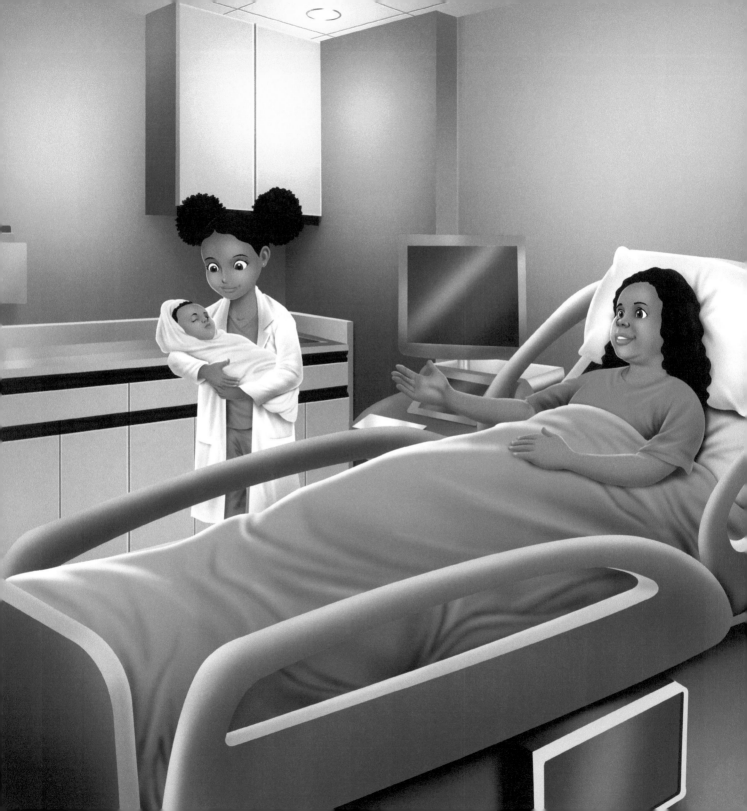

Obstetrician-gynecologists take care of babies and women. They help take care of moms when they are carrying your brother or sister in their belly and help deliver them into the world. They also help make sure women like your mom, aunt, or grandmother stay healthy.

"There sure are a lot of different kinds of doctors!" squeals Olivia.

"That's not all!" says mother.

Some doctors take care of the brain. They are called neurosurgeons. They can do brain surgery if you have a brain injury, severe headaches, or seizures where your body shakes without you telling it to do so.

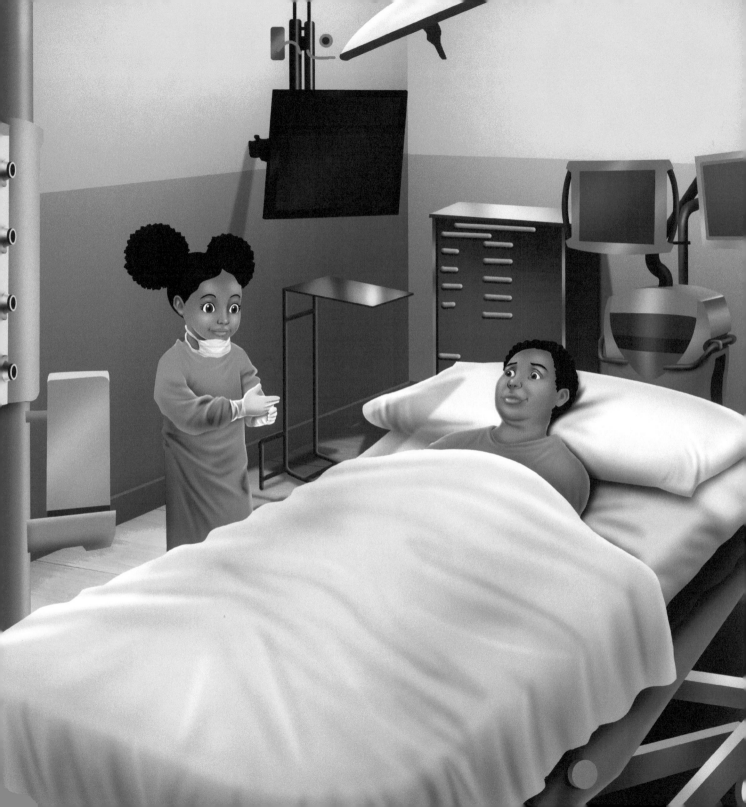

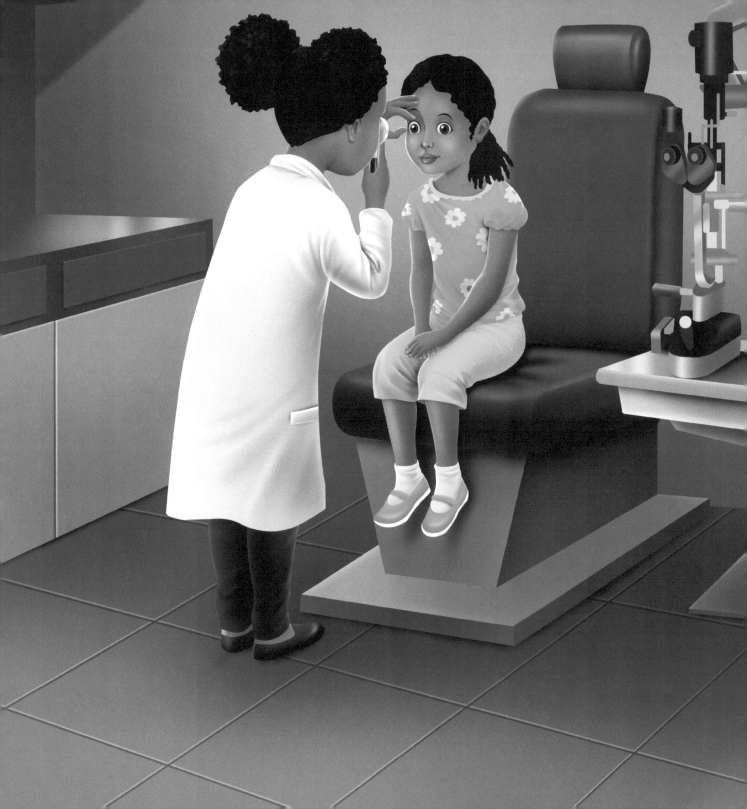

You can be an ophthalmologist. They are also called eye doctors and they take care of your eyes if you have trouble seeing or have an injury to your eyes. They also check your eyes for different diseases.

You can be a pulmonologist. They are also called lung doctors and help take care of your lungs if you have a bad cough or trouble breathing.

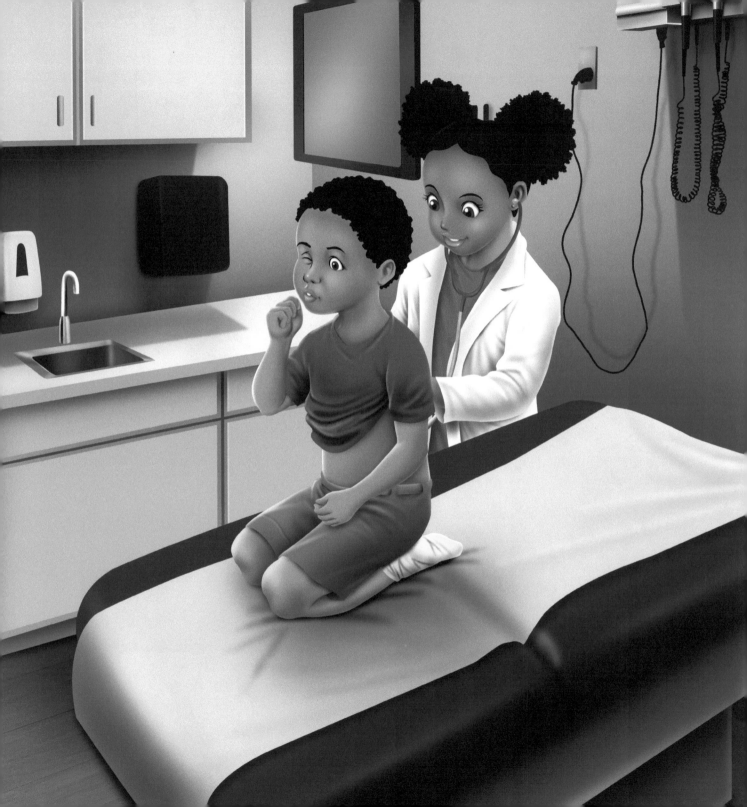

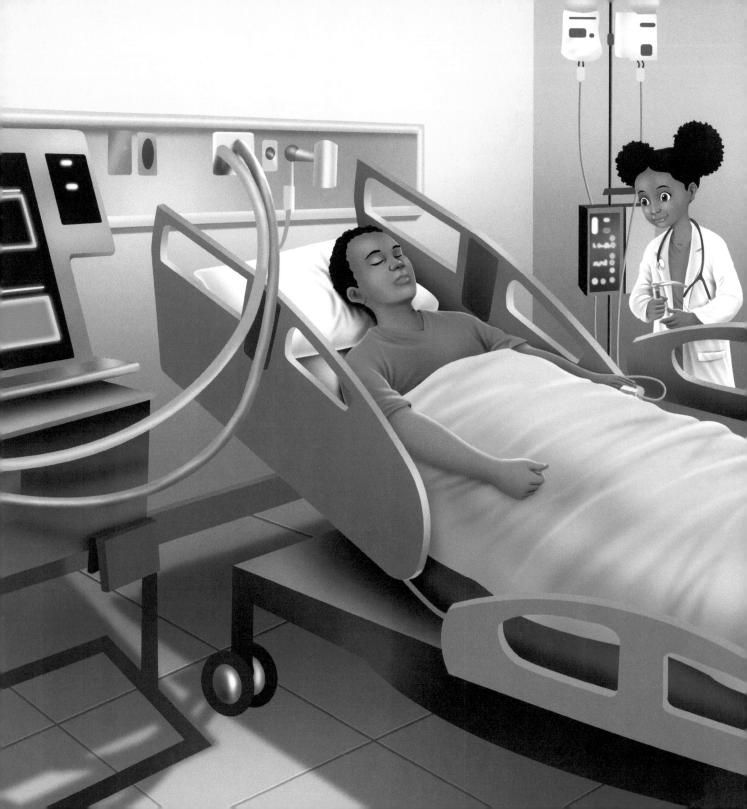

"When I had surgery, what was the name of the doctor that put me to sleep?" Olivia asked.

"Oh, the anesthesiologist sweetie," says mother.

Anesthesiologists are doctors that will put you to sleep when you have surgery, so you won't feel pain while the surgeon operates.

Pharmacists are doctors who give you medication when you are sick to make you feel better and to help keep you healthy.

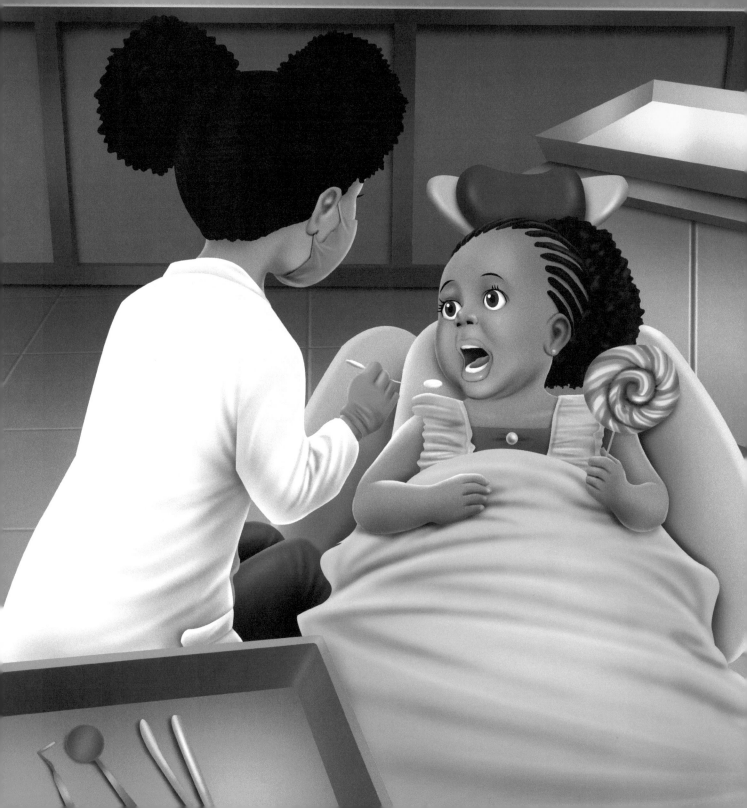

Dentist are doctors who help keep your teeth clean and keep them healthy by fixing cavities if you eat too much candy.

"WOW!" Olivia squeals with glee. "I didn't know there were so many different types of doctors!"

"Yes, my darling. There are many kinds of doctors, and you can be any one of them you want. Read lots of books and do well in school, and you can become a doctor, too," says Mother.

"Where are you going, Olivia?" Mother asks.

"I'm going to read to teddy so I can become a doctor!" Olivia says.

JUL - 1 2019

CPSIA information can be obtained
at www.ICGtesting.com
Printed in the USA
LVHW071558170719
624399LV00002B/16/P

* 9 7 8 1 9 8 5 3 9 0 3 8 6 *